FIRST
CLASS
POSTAGE
REQUIRED

"I have placed information vital to the survival of the Rebellion into the memory systems of this R2 unit. My father will know how to retrieve it. You must see this droid safely delivered to him on Alderaan. This is our most desperate hour. Help me, Obi-Wan Kenobi. You're my only hope."

STAR WARS™

PUBLISHED BY THUNDER BAY PRESS, SAN DIEGO, CA

FIRST
CLASS
POSTAGE
REQUIRED

Obi-Wan Kenobi hands Luke Skywalker his father's lightsaber, calling it "an elegant weapon for a more civilized age." Obi-Wan explains that Luke's father and other Jedi Knights were "guardians of peace and justice" in the Republic for more than a thousand generations… "Before the dark times. Before the Empire."

STAR WARS™

PUBLISHED BY THUNDER BAY PRESS, SAN DIEGO, CA

FIRST
CLASS
POSTAGE
REQUIRED

STAR WARS

Luke Skywalker and Obi-Wan Kenobi meet Han Solo and Chewbacca for the first time in a cantina in the Mos Eisley spaceport. He boasts about his ship's ability to maneuver at lightspeed through the famous Kessel Run route.

PUBLISHED BY THUNDER BAY PRESS, SAN DIEGO, CA

Luke Skywalker and Obi-Wan Kenobi hitch a ride with smuggler Han Solo and his Wookiee co-pilot, Chewbacca, on the *Millennium Falcon*. The group heads to Alderaan to deliver R2-D2 to Princess Leia's father. But the planet has been destroyed!

STAR WARS™

PUBLISHED BY THUNDER BAY PRESS, SAN DIEGO, CA

Luke Skywalker, Han Solo, and Chewbacca fight their way through the Death Star to rescue Princess Leia. But the princess is no damsel in distress. Disguised as a stormtrooper, Luke breaks Leia out of her cell. While she's grateful, it's the sharp-tongued Han Solo who eventually wins her heart.

PUBLISHED BY THUNDER BAY PRESS, SAN DIEGO, CA

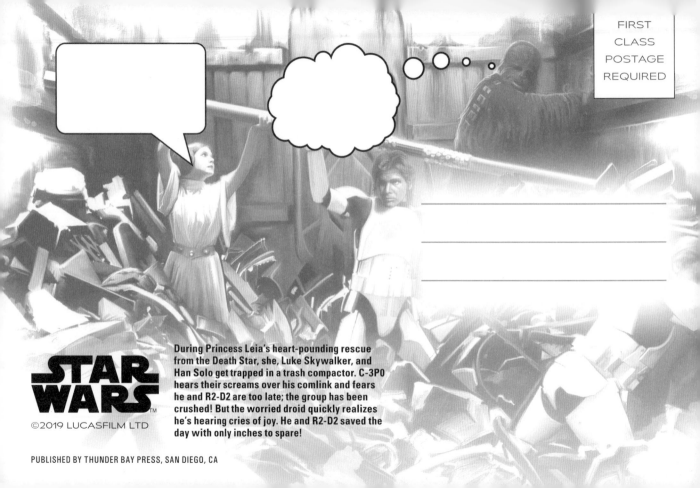

FIRST
CLASS
POSTAGE
REQUIRED

During Princess Leia's heart-pounding rescue from the Death Star, she, Luke Skywalker, and Han Solo get trapped in a trash compactor. C-3PO hears their screams over his comlink and fears he and R2-D2 are too late; the group has been crushed! But the worried droid quickly realizes he's hearing cries of joy. He and R2-D2 saved the day with only inches to spare!

STAR WARS™

PUBLISHED BY THUNDER BAY PRESS, SAN DIEGO, CA

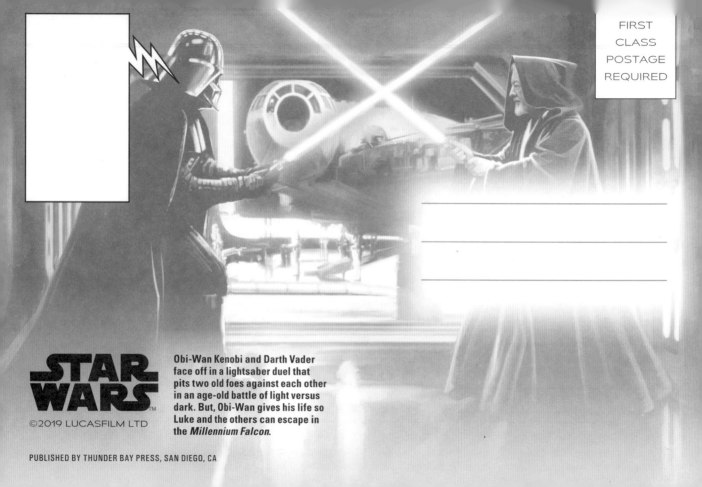

STAR WARS

Obi-Wan Kenobi and Darth Vader face off in a lightsaber duel that pits two old foes against each other in an age-old battle of light versus dark. But, Obi-Wan gives his life so Luke and the others can escape in the *Millennium Falcon*.

PUBLISHED BY THUNDER BAY PRESS, SAN DIEGO, CA

FIRST
CLASS
POSTAGE
REQUIRED

In this climactic battle, Han Solo fends off Imperial fighters, as Luke Skywalker uses the Force to help him target the Death Star's external exhaust port. Luke hits the mark and blows the evil Empire's killing machine to smithereens!

STAR WARS™

PUBLISHED BY THUNDER BAY PRESS, SAN DIEGO, CA

Luke Skywalker scans the icy slopes of the planet Hoth searching for a meteor he saw fall. What Luke doesn't know is it was no meteor; it was an Imperial probe searching for the Rebel Alliance's new base. A tauntaun (snow lizard) Luke is riding smells a wampa, a snow monster that is about to wreak havoc.

STAR WARS

©2019 LUCASFILM LTD

PUBLISHED BY THUNDER BAY PRESS, SAN DIEGO, CA

AT-AT walkers (All-Terrain, Armored Transports) move in on the Rebel forces. Luke leads his starfighter squadron on a thrilling offensive against the steel "beasts." Luke weaves his starfighter in and out of the legs of the impenetrable fighting machines.

STAR WARS

PUBLISHED BY THUNDER BAY PRESS, SAN DIEGO, CA

FIRST
CLASS
POSTAGE
REQUIRED

Luke's X-wing fighter crashes into a swamp on the planet Dagobah. There Luke begins his training with the small and eccentric Jedi master, Yoda. The teacher pushes Luke to his limits, leaving the young man wondering if he's unfit for his new role. But Yoda tells Luke to "feel the Force," then demonstrates just how powerful it is by raising Luke's X-wing out of the bog.

©2019 LUCASFILM LTD

PUBLISHED BY THUNDER BAY PRESS, SAN DIEGO, CA

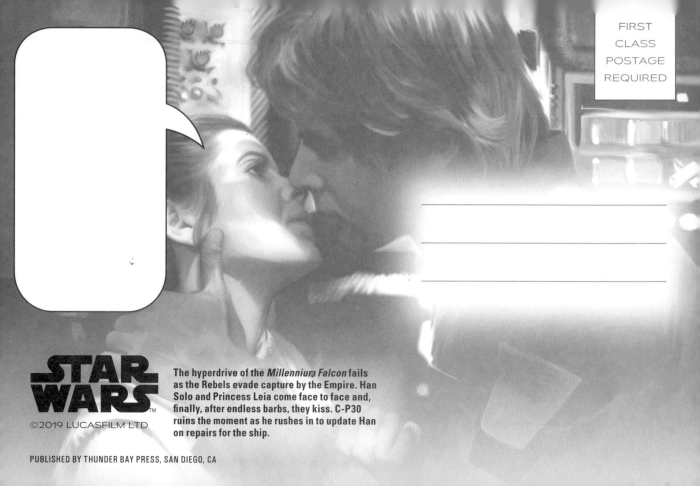

STAR WARS™

©2019 LUCASFILM LTD

The hyperdrive of the *Millennium Falcon* fails as the Rebels evade capture by the Empire. Han Solo and Princess Leia come face to face and, finally, after endless barbs, they kiss. C-P30 ruins the moment as he rushes in to update Han on repairs for the ship.

PUBLISHED BY THUNDER BAY PRESS, SAN DIEGO, CA

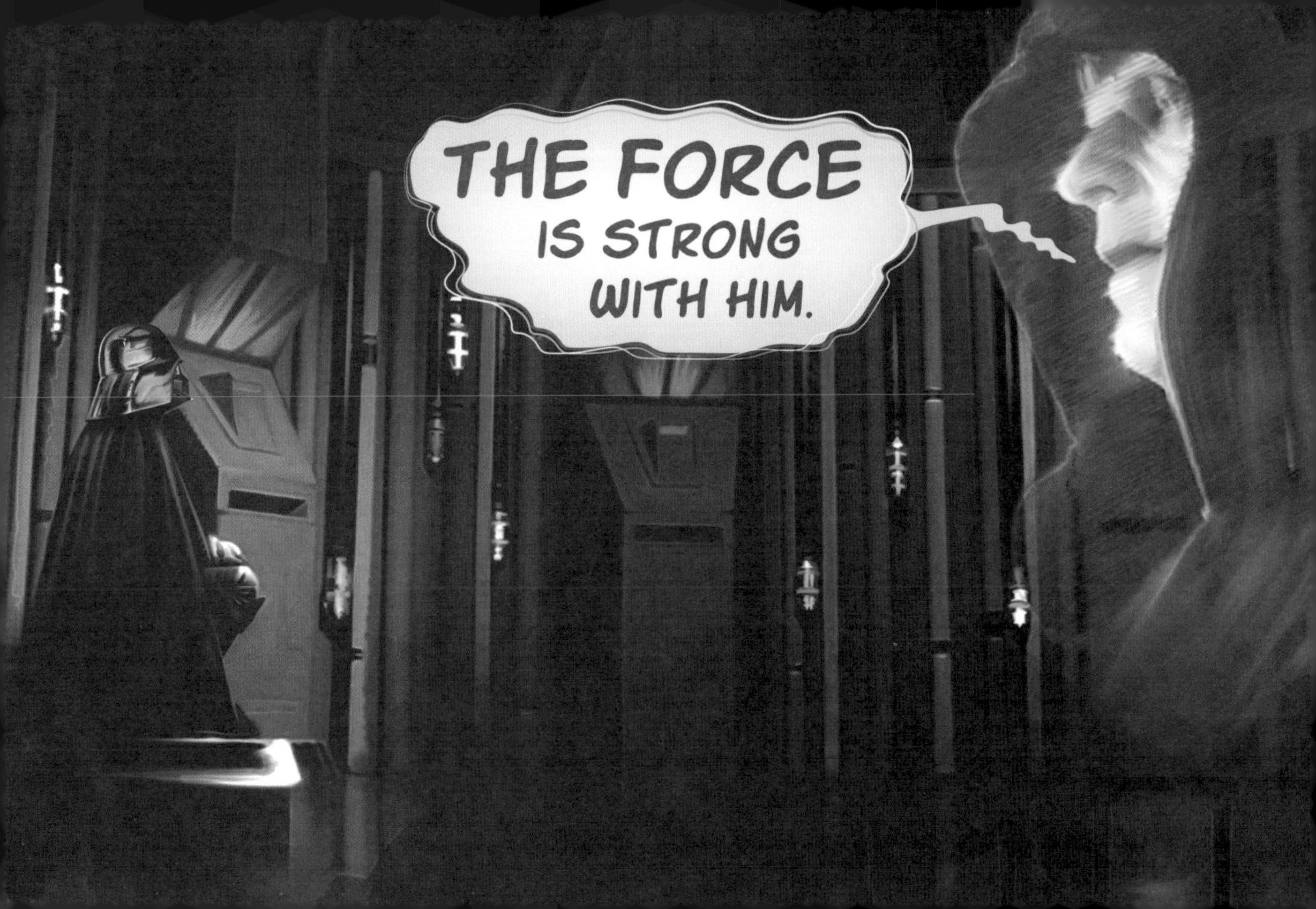
THE FORCE IS STRONG WITH HIM.

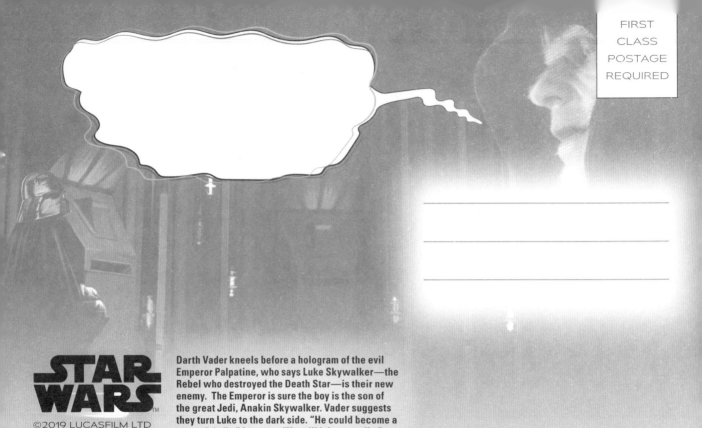

Darth Vader kneels before a hologram of the evil Emperor Palpatine, who says Luke Skywalker—the Rebel who destroyed the Death Star—is their new enemy. The Emperor is sure the boy is the son of the great Jedi, Anakin Skywalker. Vader suggests they turn Luke to the dark side. "He could become a powerful ally," he says. "He will join us or die."

©2019 LUCASFILM LTD

PUBLISHED BY THUNDER BAY PRESS, SAN DIEGO, CA

FIRST
CLASS
POSTAGE
REQUIRED

In a heart-pounding lightsaber duel above Cloud City's central airshaft, Darth Vader disarms Luke by severing his right hand. Then the Dark Lord urges Luke to join forces with him. Luke refuses, accusing Darth Vader of murdering his father. In a shocking turn, Vader reveals he is Luke's father. A horrified Luke sees no way out. He drops into the endless airshaft. He'd rather die than turn to the dark side. Miraculously, he's ejected from the bottom of the floating metropolis, managing to hang on to an antenna with his remaining hand.

STAR WARS™

©2019 LUCASFILM LTD

PUBLISHED BY THUNDER BAY PRESS, SAN DIEGO, CA

FIRST
CLASS
POSTAGE
REQUIRED

_____

_____

_____

A mysterious bounty hunter named Boushh captured Chewbacca and brought him to Jabba the Hutt. Boushh gives the gangster a price for the Wookiee. "Fifty thousand, no less." Jabba inquires why the price is so high, and is told, "Because he's holding a thermal detonator!" It turns out the bounty hunter is Princess Leia in disguise!

STAR WARS ™

©2019 LUCASFILM LTD

PUBLISHED BY THUNDER BAY PRESS, SAN DIEGO, CA

STAR WARS™

©2019 LUCASFILM LTD

Luke Skywalker confronts Jabba the Hutt, who orders his henchmen to feed Luke Skywalker to the voracious Sarlacc. But Luke and a captive Princess Leia manage to escape. They retrieve their friends and their droids and fly off to safety.

PUBLISHED BY THUNDER BAY PRESS, SAN DIEGO, CA

Luke Skywalker and the group walk into a trap as they search for Princess Leia. R2-D2 gets them out of the net, but they're surrounded by angry Ewoks. The creatures tie everyone up… except C-3PO, who they believe is a golden god. Luke calls to the droid, "Threepio, tell them if they don't do as you wish, you'll become angry and use your magic." And with that, Luke uses the Force to lift C-3PO in the air. The awestruck Ewoks set the group free and welcome them into their tribe.

PUBLISHED BY THUNDER BAY PRESS, SAN DIEGO, CA

STAR WARS™

©2019 LUCASFILM LTD

Han Solo's frenemy, Lando Calrissian, commands the *Millennium Falcon* with co-pilot, Nien Nunb. The Rebel Alliance fleet coordinates with them to launch a surprise attack on the Death Star. But the Empire is jamming their communications. It's a trap!

PUBLISHED BY THUNDER BAY PRESS, SAN DIEGO, CA